Annie Oakley
SHARPSHOOTER

BY CHARLES SPAIN VERRAL

PICTURES BY E. JOSEPH DREANY

SIMON AND SCHUSTER • NEW YORK

THIS IS A BRAND-NEW BOOK, WRITTEN AND ILLUSTRATED ESPECIALLY
FOR GOLDEN BOOKS

THE LITTLE GOLDEN BOOKS ARE PRODUCED UNDER THE SUPERVISION OF
MARY REED, Ph.D.
FORMERLY OF TEACHERS COLLEGE, COLUMBIA UNIVERSITY

Fun and adventure are never far away when Annie Oakley, cowgirl of screen and television fame, is around. In this second Annie Oakley Little Golden Book, Tagg gives a birthday party for his sister. And what a surprise party it turns out to be!

IT was Annie Oakley's birthday and she thought everybody—even her brother, Tagg—had forgotten all about it.

But Tagg hadn't. No, siree. He had a big surprise for his sister.

Right after breakfast, he saddled Pixie and rode off, calling, "Don't go away until I get back, Annie."

"I won't," Annie replied. But she was a little puzzled as to why Tagg had wanted her to stay home.

In front of the hotel, Tagg met Lofty, the deputy sheriff, and a whole crowd of people—almost everybody in town.

"Annie's at home," Tagg said. "Are you all ready?"

"We will be by the time you bring her out there," Lofty said. He turned to the crowd. "I've told you the plan, folks. While Tagg goes after Annie, let's move."

As Tagg started away he saw two strangers back of the crowd. He wondered who they were. And he wondered even more when he heard one of them say, "Let's follow these folks, Pete. They'll lead us to Annie Oakley."

"Okay, Nick," the other man said. "Our job is to get her. Hope we won't have any trouble."

Tagg didn't like the sound of what he'd overheard. Annie had helped Lofty in running down outlaws. And maybe these men were friends of one of those outlaws and were planning to harm his sister. He'd have to warn her.

But he decided to wait until after the surprise.

Annie was really puzzled when Tagg told her that somebody wanted to see her out at the fair grounds and to ask no questions. But she swung up on Target and went along.

When they got to the fair grounds, there was nobody in sight.

"Is this a joke?" Annie asked. "I don't see anybody."

Suddenly from behind the bandstand and other

buildings came many people. And in front was the baker holding up a big cake with one lighted candle on it.

"Happy birthday, Annie!" everybody shouted. "Surprise! Surprise!"

"I didn't know how old you were, Annie," laughed the baker, "that's why I just put one extra-large candle on the cake."

Well, it *was* a real surprise party and Annie was happy. Folks began giving her presents, all kinds of presents. Even little old Miss Graham, who had taught Annie in school, drove up in a wagon and handed Annie a gift.

And right away Annie began opening the presents. She was very excited.

A breeze was blowing the wrappings every which way and Tagg busied himself picking up the papers. All of a sudden he noticed that the two strangers had arrived and were watching Annie.

"I'd better warn her right now," Tagg thought.

But at that very moment, a large piece of paper blew right into the faces of the team hitched to Miss Graham's wagon.

The horses were scared. They reared—and then they bolted!

Miss Graham couldn't hold them and she screamed, "Help! Help!"

Tagg was close by and, with a leap, he managed to pull himself up on the back of the swaying wagon.

He scrambled to the driver's seat beside Miss Graham
and seized the reins. He pulled on them hard. But he
couldn't stop the horses.

Annie saw what had happened. She was on Target
in a flash and rode as hard as she could. For the run-
away horses were heading straight for the railroad
tracks—and a train was coming.

In a burst of speed, Annie drew alongside. She sprang from the saddle and landed right on the back of one of the horses.

As the crowd of people breathlessly watched, Annie swerved the team away from the railroad tracks, just as the train thundered past!

U. S.1113270

A shout went up from the on-lookers. Men rushed to help Annie stop the horses.

When the team was quieted and Miss Graham helped down, Tagg turned to his sister.

"Annie!" he said. "You were wonderful!"

"And you were a brave boy to do what you did," Annie said. "I think you deserve an extra-large piece of my birthday cake."

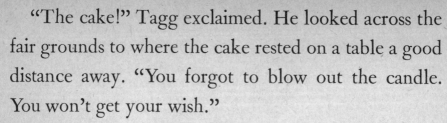

"The cake!" Tagg exclaimed. He looked across the fair grounds to where the cake rested on a table a good distance away. "You forgot to blow out the candle. You won't get your wish."

"I'll take care of that right now," Annie said.

She mounted Target and called, "Everybody out of the way, please!"

The crowd parted so that there was a clear space between Annie and the cake.

Then Annie galloped toward the cake, raised her gun, and took quick aim.

Crack! went her gun.

Pow! went the bullet dead on its target.

The two strangers stared in amazement.

"Did you see that?" one of them said. "She shot out the flame of the candle from way over there!"

"What a sharpshooter—as well as a trick rider!" the other man said. "We've got to get her!"

Tagg was alarmed when he saw the two men come up to his sister.

"Look out, Annie," he said. "They're coming to get you!"

"We certainly are, Miss Oakley," one of them said.

"We would like you to appear in our Wild West show at the state fair," the other man added. "With that wonderful riding and sharpshooting, you'll be our star attraction. It's a benefit performance."

Tagg's mouth dropped open. So these men weren't outlaws after all. They were from a Wild West show! This *was* a surprise party!

"I'd be glad to help out," Annie said. "But first, let's cut the cake and everybody have a piece."

Well, when the day came, Annie appeared in the Wild West show at the fair. And she took Tagg along.

People thronged to see her ride and shoot and rope. She was the star attraction.

And Tagg thought that this was Annie's nicest birthday present of all.